PYTHOR'S REVENGE

By Meredith Rusu

SCHOLASTIC INC.

The publisher does not have any control over and does not assume any responsibility for author or third-party websites or their content.

This book is a work of fiction. Names, characters, places, and incidents are either the product of the author's imagination or are used fictitiously, and any resemblance to actual persons, living or dead, business establishments, events, or locales is entirely coincidental.

ISBN 978-1-338-11796-7

10 9 8 7   19 20 21

Printed in the U.S.A.   40
First printing 2017

FROM THE JOURNAL OF

Master Wu

**W**hat makes the most dangerous enemy?

Is it the opponent who battles with great strength — like the relentless stone and skeleton warriors? Or is it the cunning foe with unmatched intelligence, such as the Nindroids and Anacondrai?

Perhaps the most dangerous enemy is the one whose quest for power is all-consuming — the Overlords and Master Chens of our realm.

Indeed, there are many types of enemies. And the ninja have faced them all. But it is

difficult to say which were the *most* dangerous. Each posed their own challenges and stretched the ninja to their true potential.

Some enemies were vanquished. Others were banished to the Cursed Realm. And then there were the rare few who transformed from enemies into allies, such as Master Yang.

Master Yang used to be a wise teacher. But his spirit became trapped in the Temple of Airjitzu, cursed to remain there for all time. Over the centuries, he became vengeful.

When the day of the Yin-Yang Eclipse fell on the Day of the Departed, Master Yang saw his opportunity. He unleashed the spirits of the ninjas' former adversaries to do battle. Master Chen, Kozu, and even Cryptor all returned for one fateful evening to exact revenge.

But Cole discovered that Master Yang was not truly evil. He was simply a forgotten soul

4

who longed to be remembered. Cole helped Yang realize he was already remembered as the creator of Airjitzu. In return, Master Yang allowed Cole to pass through the Yin-Yang portal in his place. Cole became flesh and blood once again.

Reunited, the ninja are prepared to face whatever enemies await them. Which brings me back to my original question — what makes the most dangerous enemy?

It could be argued that the ninja have already overcome the most dangerous foes possible, and that any challenge left for them to face would simply be a repeat.

And yet . . . perhaps that is my answer. The most dangerous enemy is not the one who is completely unexpected. No, it is the one who keeps coming *back* time and again, never relinquishing the fight.

Though the ninja have defeated many

opponents, there are those who have managed to slither away undetected, waiting for their moment to rise again. I hope the ninja are ready for such enemies. Because there is no telling what they will have learned with the advantage of time . . .

Chapter 1

Was I right, or was I right?" Cole smiled triumphantly as he guided the other ninja into the courtyard of the Temple of Airjitzu. He and his friends all held softly glowing Day of the Departed lanterns.

"I told you guys," Cole continued. "This will be the perfect place for us to train!"

The friends admired the nighttime beauty of the ancient temple. It had been returned to its former glory in the wake of their battle against Master Yang. Now its towers rose tall and pristine against the starry night sky — a vision of how it had been long ago.

Cole smiled and glanced up to one of the temple towers. He caught a glimpse of Master Yang smiling from a window. Only Cole knew that the master's spirit remained inside. But Yang was no longer vengeful. Cole had set him free from that fate. Now Yang's spirit would remain as a guide, watching students practice the Airjitzu fighting style he had invented many years ago. Yang was not forgotten with time. Instead, he was cherished.

Yang winked at Cole, and Cole winked back.

"Happy Day of the Departed, ninja," said Master Wu.

"Happy Day of the Departed, Master," they replied. Then they yawned and stretched.

"I don't know about you guys," said Kai, "but I could use a good night's sleep. All this battling has gotten me drained, departed-style."

"I agree," said Zane. "A full night's rest would be restorative."

"Let's head back to the *Bounty*," said Lloyd. "We can start packing up everything to move into the temple tomorrow."

"Ugh, *tomorrow*?" groaned Jay. "Can't we take a day to relax?"

"What did you have in mind?" asked Nya.

"I don't know," said Jay. "A video game tournament. Maybe eat my way through all the Day of the Departed candy I collected. Ooh, ooh, guys, I'll bet my mom still has some crumb cake left —"

Just then, Lloyd's cell phone buzzed. "Huh," said Lloyd. "I just got a text from Dareth."

"What's it say?" asked Kai.

Lloyd read from his phone. " *'Do u guys (plus grl) have plans 4 tmrw? Have something fun in mind.'* "

"See?!" Jay exclaimed. "Even Dareth knows we could use some fun!"

Lloyd shrugged. "I guess one day off couldn't hurt."

The others nodded. So Lloyd texted Dareth back.

"No plans. What's up?"

Three dots appeared on Lloyd's phone screen, indicating Dareth was typing.

"Meet me at the Ninjago Museum of History. Tmrw morning, before opening. Will show u then."

"Guys... this does *not* look like fun." Jay frowned as they arrived at the Ninjago Museum of History the next morning.

Scattered all around the front entrance were piles of debris. And leading straight into the museum storage room was... a hole in the wall shaped like Kozu, the Stone Warrior.

"My favorite ninja!" cried Dareth, stepping through the hole. "Right on time, as always."

"Dareth, what happened?" asked Lloyd. "Why is there a hole in the museum wall?"

"And why is it shaped like Kozu?" Nya added.

"Ah, crazy story," said Dareth. "You know how on the Day of the Departed we honor, well, the departed?"

"Let me guess," said Kai. "You encountered an *actual* departed enemy from the past who wanted to send you to the Departed Realm in his place?"

"No, that's not . . . oh, yeah, that *is* it, actually," said Dareth. He looked slightly deflated that Kai had guessed the truth so easily. But he bounced back quickly. "Naturally, he was no match for the Brown Ninja. I outsmarted him with my usual combination of skill and astonishing quick thinking. However, the battle had some, er, side effects."

"We can see that," said Nya. "It looks like Dr. Saunders's museum needs major repairs."

Jay shook his head. "I don't understand. You texted us saying you had something fun in mind. What does this have to do with fun?"

"Well, if there's one thing I know about my ninja, it's that you guys *love* fixing things," said Dareth. "Fixing Ninjago City. Fixing the realms. I figured that this sort of laid-back, low-key fixing would be right up your alley."

The ninja blinked.

"Are you serious?" exclaimed Kai. "Spinjitzu is fun. Kicking Master Chen's butt is fun. But cleaning up your mess is *not* fun!"

"Why don't *you* help Dr. Saunders clean his museum?" asked Cole.

Dareth sighed heavily. "I would if I could, little ninja. But there's so much to do and so little time."

"Such as . . . ?" asked Kai.

"The BorgWatch unveiling!" exclaimed Dareth. "I've been waiting months for the big reveal. I've followed every chirp, every media leak, every photo-chat. All the intel is pointing to a release this week. Maybe even today! I have to be ready, and I can't be ready if I'm sweeping up stone warrior dust."

"Let me get this straight," said Nya. "You want *us* to clean up *your* mess because you have to wait outside the Borg Store on the *chance* the BorgWatch might be unveiled?"

Dareth nodded. "I knew you'd understand."

Nya looked like she was ready to show Dareth just how much she did *not* understand, but Lloyd held her back. "Guys, this is serious. Dr. Saunders needs our help."

"Speaking of . . ." said Lloyd.

Everyone looked over to see a very distressed Dr. Sander Saunders, the head of the Ninjago Museum of History, rushing toward them.

"Ninja, thanks to the goodness that you are here!" Dr. Saunders cried in his thick

accent. "My beautiful museum! Do you see what has been happening? Stone... debris... HOLE! This must to be fixed. Right away!"

Dareth patted Kai on the back. "Like I said, nobody is better at fixing things than you guys. Plus girl." He quickly stepped away. "Gotta go."

The ninja watched in disbelief as Dareth took off down the museum steps. Then they turned to the doctor.

"Uh, Dr. Saunders," said Lloyd, "let's talk about all this for a minute."

"Here, let's go inside," said Jay. He guided the shaking doctor through the Kozu-shaped hole. "Right this way."

Chapter 2

No, no, no." Dr. Saunders groaned as he surveyed the damage. "My display hall, my storage room. All broken, very bad. But why? Why? What made all this happen?"

"Well . . ." Jay started.

"As you know, there was a Yin-Yang Eclipse last night," said Zane.

"And the spirits of our old enemies kind of inhabited the statues from your Hall of Villainy," said Cole.

"And came back to battle us for one night," finished Nya.

Dr. Saunders shook his head. "You speak, but I do not understand. The statues, what made them move? *Why* did they move?"

"Well, why is kind of a long story," said Jay. "But they did move. And one of them attacked Dareth in your storage room."

"The big stone guy," added Kai. "The one who left behind his hole in the wall."

Dr. Saunders moaned. "This is bad, yes, very, very bad. Everything took a long time to create, you see. All the statues, painted by hand. Special-ordered months in advance."

"Hey, it's okay, doc," said Jay. "It's just a little messy. Nothing a few mops and buckets can't clean up." As he spoke, he leaned against a statue of a Nindroid. One of its arms fell off and smashed to the ground.

"Everything you are doing is bad," said Dr. Saunders. "I want you to know this."

"Do not worry, doctor," said Zane. "We will help you to fix your museum so it's back to optimal conditions."

"Optimal conditions..." Dr. Saunders's eyes suddenly went wide. "Oh, dear, oh, dear, oh dear, oh dear, oh dear!"

The doctor rushed behind several dusty shelves. A moment later, the ninja heard him cry out.

"Dr. Saunders, are you okay?" Cole exclaimed as they all chased after him.

When the ninja turned the corner, they discovered Dr. Saunders with his head in his hands. He was standing next to a broken device hanging from the wall. "Destroyed! Shattered! Yes! Completely ruined!" he cried.

"What was this?" Nya asked, stepping forward.

"It appears to have been an internal systematic temperature gauge," said Zane, scanning the debris.

"An internal whosit whatsit?" asked Jay.

"A thermostat," explained Zane.

"Ah," said Jay. Then he raised an eyebrow at the weeping museum director. "Gee, I

would have expected something more... dramatic."

But Dr. Saunders shook his head. "One of a kind. This thermostat was very precise, you see. I have been tinkering with it for years. To keep the base — I mean, the museum — at perfect temperature. For customer comfort, you understanding."

"Here, maybe we can fix it," said Kai, reaching toward the shattered device.

An odd look passed across Dr. Saunders's face. He smacked Kai's hand away.

"Sorry," said Kai, stunned. "I was just trying to help."

"No, no, no help. It is requiring very specific parts," Dr. Saunders explained.

"What if we could find replacements for the parts that were broken?" offered Lloyd. "We happen to know a guy who might have just what you need."

"Ah, yes, Dr. Cyrus Borg." Zane smiled. "He

would indeed have everything needed to repair the thermostat. Perhaps improve it."

"Dr. Borg, you are saying?" Dr. Saunders suddenly sounded curious. "Interesting. Precise temperature control, very impressive. Yes, it would be the perfect . . . time."

"Right . . ." said Cole. "So, we'll go see Dr. Borg, then, and ask if he has the part you need to fix your thermostat?"

Dr. Saunders didn't reply. He simply gazed into the distance.

Lloyd looked at his friends and shrugged. "I'll take that as a 'yes.'"

The ninja stepped out from the dark museum into the bright sunlight.

"Do you think Borg will have what we need?" Kai asked Lloyd. "His expertise isn't exactly heating-and-cooling repair."

"I can't imagine he wouldn't," said Lloyd. "Dr. Borg has everything."

The sunshine was suddenly blocked by an enormous shadow overhead. The ninja looked up to see a giant blimp floating in the sky.

"Coming soon!" a loudspeaker from the blimp announced. *"The new BorgWatch! Guaranteed to change the way you tell time . . . forever!"*

A big smile popped up on Jay's face. "Now THAT'S something worth getting excited about. I can't *wait* for the new BorgWatch! All of Borg's gadgets are so cool!"

"It sounds like you should get in line right behind Dareth," Nya teased.

"Hey, if I could, I would," said Jay. "This was *supposed* to be our day off."

"The BorgWatch is predicted to be revolutionary," Zane interjected. "A seamless merger of technology and fashion."

"What he said." Jay pointed at Zane. "Seriously, the BorgWatch is going to be the biggest thing to hit Ninjago City since, well, the BorgPad! And the BorgPod."

"Don't forget the Cyrus PDA," added Cole.

Jay sighed. "Dr. Saunders got all weepy over his broken thermostat. That's weird, right? It's just a thermostat. But I have to admit I may weep with joy when that BorgWatch is finally unveiled."

"Maybe we can get a sneak peek." Lloyd smiled at Jay. "You know, have some fun today after all."

"What do you mean?" Jay asked curiously.

"While we're stopping by Cyrus Borg's, it can't hurt to ask if we can take a look at the BorgWatch prototype," Lloyd explained. "You know, as a favor."

Jay's eyes grew wide. "Do you . . . do you really think . . . OHMYGOSH!"

"It's worth a shot," said Lloyd. "And if he says 'no,' we still need the parts for Dr. Saunders's thermostat."

"Then it is settled," said Zane. "To the Borg Store."

The ninja kept chatting as they headed farther down the street, away from the blimp. None of them noticed the lone shadow that remained behind in a nearby alleyway.

The shadow's owner watched the ninja intently for a moment. Then he silently slithered away.

Chapter 3

My good friends, what a pleasant surprise!" Dr. Cyrus Borg wheeled up to greet the ninja as they entered the Borg Store. All around him, workers scurried to and fro, setting up the store for the upcoming BorgWatch reveal.

"You are looking as well as ever," Borg said, smiling. "Ah, and Cole, I see you have rejoined us in the world of the living. Perhaps an even pleasanter surprise."

"Thanks, Dr. Borg," Cole replied. "I've never felt better."

"I apologize; the store is in a frenzy." Cyrus Borg gestured to the flurry of activity around him. "I'm sure you've seen the ads. My new BorgWatch is causing quite the hubbub."

"I'll say." Kai peeked through thick curtains shielding the store windows from the outside street. Hordes of people were camped outside, awaiting the big BorgWatch reveal. Kai caught a glimpse of Dareth toward the back of the line.

"It was a challenge just to get in here," Kai continued. "It's a good thing you let us in the back. Those campers wouldn't take too kindly to us cutting the line."

"Indeed not." Dr. Borg couldn't help beaming. "It's all very exciting. The release of a new gadget is always buzzworthy, but this is perhaps my biggest achievement yet!"

"If I might ask, Dr. Borg," said Zane, "what makes the BorgWatch so different from a standard timepiece?"

Borg's eyes flashed gleefully. "Oh, my dear Zane, it is *so* much more than a time-piece. The BorgWatch will revolutionize the smart device industry entirely! It will provide a whole new perspective on the world as we know it . . . on the time that we live in."

Jay jumped up and down a little. "Oh, man! Can we have a sneak peek? Please, doctor? Pretty, pretty, *pretty* please???"

Borg hesitated. "I'm afraid that won't be possible . . ."

"Can't you make an exception for us, just this once?" asked Lloyd.

"We are your biggest fans," said Kai.

"And, not to bring it up, but we did kind of save Borg Industries from the Nindroids a while back," said Cole.

"And the Digital Overlord," added Zane.

"And the Anacondrai and ghosts," said Nya. "Basically, its general existence is thanks to us."

"So what do you say?" Lloyd gave Cyrus Borg his most charming smile. "A return favor for some old friends?"

The doctor looked torn. "I-I don't mean to sound ungrateful. But I simply can't reveal the watch ahead of, well, the reveal. These unveilings are quite sensitive. Contracts have been signed. Nondisclosures negotiated years in advance. It would put me in an extremely awkward position."

The ninja sighed.

"Well, you can't blame us for trying," said Lloyd. "Speaking of trying, we're actually here to ask another favor."

Alarm crossed the doctor's face again.

"No, no," said Lloyd. "Nothing confidential. We were just hoping you could give us some parts to repair a very sensitive thermostat. One that needs to keep a precise temperature at all times. We kind of destroyed the Ninjago Museum of History's thermostat."

"And by 'we,' he means Dareth," said Nya.

"Ah, I see," said Borg. He tapped his fingers together pensively. "My, my, that *is* a coincidence. The BorgWatch is one thing, but surely this would be permitted? Should I ... do I dare ... ? Oh, my, I just can't resist! I know after all I just said, I shouldn't be telling you this, but I believe I have *exactly* what you are looking for."

"Really?" Lloyd asked hopefully.

"Yes," said Dr. Borg. "A precise temperature gauge just happens to be one of the many revolutionary components of the BorgWatch."

"The BorgWatch has a temperature gauge?!" Jay squealed. "Awesome!"

"Why would a watch need that?" Nya asked, confused.

"To regulate optimal body temperature!" cried the doctor. "It's another example of how this device will change the way we *live*. Now, I can't show you the watch itself. But I can help you with your temperature problem."

Borg wheeled behind a locked case com-pletely shrouded in velvet. He ducked behind it and began punching in a code. Every so often, he'd peek up to make sure no one was watching. When he was done, he closed the case door and wheeled back out.

"Behold, ninja, the revolution of modern-day living," he declared.

The ninja caught their breath as the doc-tor held up what looked like . . .

. . . a metal toothpick.

"Is . . . is that . . ." said Jay. "Uh, what is that?"

"The BorgWatch Thermodynamic Tem-perature Gauge, of course!" cried Borg. "Able to monitor and advise precise temperature conditions for optimal performance."

"Huh," said Jay, looking at it closely. "Does it also promote dental hygiene?"

"No, no." Borg laughed. "That would just be silly." Then his face grew serious. "Now, I am bending the rules by giving this to you ahead of time. I do have you to thank for the

continued existence of Borg Industries. And, well, let it never be said that Cyrus Borg doesn't understand the social convention of a 'return favor.'"

The doctor clapped his hands, and a half dozen assistants appeared behind him, all carrying paperwork.

"So, if you six will please just sign these nondisclosure agreements guaranteeing you won't reveal *anything* to the general public about the BorgWatch Thermodynamic Temperature Gauge ahead of the unveiling, we'll be all set."

"You need us to sign contracts?" Lloyd asked, flipping through the sixty-page document.

"No, no," Borg assured them. "Just a few short nondisclosure agreements."

"All for a toothpick?" asked Jay.

Cyrus Borg adjusted his glasses. "Well, it's a pretty life-changing 'toothpick.'"

Chapter 4

I **still don't get why we had to** sign all those papers," Kai complained as they headed back to the museum. He held the BorgWatch Thermodynamic Temperature Gauge up toward the sky, allowing the sun to glint off of it. "I mean, it's not like anyone would even *know* what this was if they saw it."

Just then, Kai stumbled on a crack in the sidewalk. The temperature gauge flew from his fingers.

"Hey, careful with that!" cried Jay, catching it. "I'm pretty sure I just signed away my family inheritance to protect this thing. Plus, it's cool."

"But what does it *do*?" Kai asked.

"The BorgWatch Thermodynamic Temperature Gauge is actually extraordinarily advanced," said Zane, scanning the metal toothpick. "It is currently calculating all our internal body temperatures and determining adjustments needed for optimal performance."

"Seriously?" asked Kai. "What's it say about me?"

Zane processed the readings. "It says you are too hot."

"That sounds about right." Nya giggled.

"Whatever." Kai slicked back his hair. "I don't need a fancy BorgWatch thermo-gizmo to tell me I'm on *fi-ya*. Come on, let's get this over to Dr. Saunders so we can take the rest of the day off —"

Suddenly, his path was blocked by a cloaked figure.

"*Ninjaaaaaa . . .*" the figure hissed.

"Uh, guys," said Jay. "Did any of you order a super-creepy escort to walk us back to the museum?"

"Who are you?" demanded Lloyd.

The figure laughed. "Please, Lloyd, don't say you've already forgotten me."

The figure lowered his hood to reveal . . . Pythor!

"Pythor?!" the ninja all cried together.

"You want to fight us *again*?" asked Lloyd. Pythor was the only true surviving Anacondrai, and a longtime enemy of the ninja. They had already defeated him on at least three occasions.

"Like father, like son," hissed Pythor. "Don't you ever learn, boy? A true enemy grows from his mistakes and changes his tactics. No, I don't have any intention of fighting you."

"Then what is your intention?" asked Zane.

Pythor smiled an impossibly large, toothy

smile. "I simply want the recognition that is mine. That I *deserve*."

"By taking over the world?" Lloyd challenged. "We're not going to let you do that."

"But that's what I've learned," said Pythor. "I don't need to take over the world in order to command its attention."

Pythor lashed out with his staff at an unsuspecting Jay. Startled, Jay stumbled back, dropping the BorgWatch temperature gauge.

Pythor whipped his long snake tail out to catch the device before it hit the pavement. "Why battle for recognition when I can simply steal it?" he said triumphantly.

"Hey!" yelled Jay. "Give that back! We promised Cyrus Borg we wouldn't let anyone see that!"

Pythor laughed. "Well, that's the icing on the cake. Of course, when I overheard your discussion outside the museum, I was hoping for an actual BorgWatch. But I suppose

this little gem of technology will have to do. Soon, I will have the whole world's attention — as the snake who revealed the first BorgWatch secret to the masses! And then I will have influence throughout the realms . . ."

"Pythor, I do not believe you have thought this through," said Zane matter-of-factly. "If your intention is to gain fame from the temperature gauge, there is a 97.8 percent chance of failure based upon my mathematical calculations."

"What he means," said Kai, "is that no one cares about a metal toothpick."

Pythor sneered. "Then you won't try and stop me."

Quickly, the Anacondrai slithered into a side alley and out of sight.

"Guys, we have to stop him!" exclaimed Jay.

"Is it really that big a deal?" asked Cole. "I mean, sure, we can't fix Dr. Saunders's thermostat now. But what harm can Pythor do with *that*?"

"We made a promise to Cyrus Borg," said Lloyd. "We can't let him down."

"Lloyd's right," said Nya.

Zane nodded solemnly. "Yes, we must keep our promise. And there is something else, too. If that temperature gauge is revealed to the public before the unveiling, we could face fines, punishment, and even jail time."

"You're telling me we could go to *jail* if a metal toothpick got revealed to the public?!" Cole exclaimed.

Zane nodded. "Yes."

The ninja all looked at one another.

"We have to stop him!" they cried at the same time. *"Ninja-GO!"*

Chapter 5

The ninja raced after Pythor. But the sneaky snake had a good head start. Pythor slithered down a narrow alleyway and around a corner.

"He may have the advantage in tight spaces," said Kai. "But he can't do this. *Ninja-GO!*"

In a red whirlwind, Kai used Airjitzu to fly up and over the buildings lining the alleyway. He landed on the other side—right in front of Pythor!

"Sorry to burst your bubble," Kai said to

Pythor. "But your fifteen minutes of fame are already up."

"That's what you think." Pythor sneered. He lashed out with his tail, knocking over a nearby stack of water barrels. The tower teetered . . . and fell straight toward Kai!

"Kai — look out!" cried Nya. Fortunately for Kai, his friends had followed him.

Using her elemental power, Nya made the water inside the barrels surge, shattering the barrels before they could crush Kai. Instead of being smashed, Kai just got drenched in a wave of water.

"Thanks, sis," said Kai. "But next time, maybe wave the water away from me instead of over me."

Nya shrugged. "Zane said you needed to cool down."

"Enough chitchat," Lloyd interrupted. "Where did Pythor go?"

The ninja looked around. Pythor had vanished!

"How did he sneak away without us seeing?" Cole asked in disbelief.

"Look — there!" cried Jay. He pointed to a barrel, still intact, rolling away. The ninja caught just a glimpse of Pythor's tail poking out through the lid before it rolled around another corner.

"That snake's not getting away so easily," Cole said. "Come on!"

The ninja used Airjitzu to spin up and over the building again. But this time, when they landed, they had a new problem.

"Whoa — hey, watch it!" Jay cried as several people shoved him away from the spot where he'd landed.

"No cutting!" the people yelled back.

"If you're here for the BorgWatch, you have to get in line like everyone else," a woman yelled at them.

The ninja looked at one another, worried. They'd landed right in the middle of the BorgWatch fans!

That meant Pythor had the secret BorgWatch Thermodynamic Temperature Gauge in his possession — and he was smack in the heart of the crowd that would want to see it most.

Pythor chuckled as his barrel rolled to a stop among the crowd of eager BorgWatch fans.

"That was too easy," he said to himself. "Why have I been fighting the ninja all this time when all I needed to do was steal the spotlight from some hotshot tech guru with low-grade security standards?"

Pythor slipped out of the crowd and looked back. There was a sea of people between him and the Borg Store — all waiting anxiously on the chance Cyrus Borg might unveil the watch today.

"I could just show them my treasure now and claim my rightful recognition," Pythor

mused. He paused. "But I am an Anacondrai. And a snake is true to his own kind. The first ones I will reveal this technological delight to will be my own brethren — the Serpentine!"

Pythor laughed and flipped up a manhole cover. He slithered down into the tunnels beneath Ninjago City, where the Serpentine lived.

Pythor disappeared just as the ninja came rushing out of the crowd.

"Dareth!" Kai exclaimed, spotting the Brown Ninja nearby in the line. "Have you seen Pythor?"

"Pythor?" Dareth asked. "Sorry, little ninja, but this Borg Industries fan has eyes for only one thing right now — the BorgWatch reveal."

"I heard it can walk your dog using a remote-controlled leash," said a nearby fan sitting in a foldout chair. "Can you imagine? Never having to walk your dog again!"

"Well, *I* heard that it can clean your house *and* cook your dinner, all while playing smooth jazz," another woman gushed.

Nya rolled her eyes. "Don't you guys think you're setting your expectations a little too high? It's just a watch."

At that, every fan in earshot gasped. *"JUST A WATCH?!"* they cried.

A man glared at her. "If by 'just a watch' you mean 'the greatest thing to happen EVER IN THE HISTORY OF THE REALMS, then yeah, I suppose it's *just a watch*."

"Look, ninja pals," Dareth whispered. "I love that you stopped by to visit, but I think you'd better keep it moving. These fans are rabid, and there's only so much I, the Brown Ninja, can do to protect you."

Then he turned back to the crowd. "She was just kidding! She's a newbie to the Borg-Tech world." He lowered his voice. "I don't think she even *knows* what a Cyrus PDA is."

"Ohh," the crowd sighed sympathetically.

Nya was about to retort when Jay quickly took her arm.

"Come on," he said. "For once I think Dareth's right. We should keep moving."

As soon as they were safely away from the crowd, Zane got his friends' attention. "I'm afraid these recent developments are concerning," he said. "Based on the fans' enthusiasm, I now calculate a 77 percent chance that revealing the BorgWatch Thermodynamic Temperature Gauge *would* bring Pythor unrivalled attention and popularity."

"We've got to find him," said Lloyd. "If he didn't show it to the fans outside the store, who is he planning to show it to?"

Cole eyed a nearby manhole cover that had shifted slightly out of place. "Maybe he wanted to start a little closer to home."

Chapter 6

The doors to the Serpentine village opened slowly.

"Skales, my long-lost friend," crooned Pythor. "How good to see you."

Pythor stood at the entrance to the underground tunnel home of the Serpentine. After the battle with the stone warriors, all the snakes lived a peaceful life down here, far away from the surface dwellers.

"What do you want, Pythor?" Skales hissed. "We're not accusssstomed to visssitors."

"My, my, is that any way to treat a guest?"

Pythor slid past him and into the village. "Especially one who comes bearing gifts?"

"I didn't think we'd be *ssse*eing you again." Skales followed him. "Not after Mas*sss*ter Chen and his Anacondrai warriors attacked Ninjago City."

"Pish-posh." Pythor waved away the comment. "Those were fake Anacondrai. I am the only *real* Anacondrai left. And when I happened to come across a rather unique commodity, I said to myself, 'Pythor P. Chumsworth, who should you show this rare treasure to first?' Naturally, I decided my fellow snakes should have the honor."

"We're no longer interested in the riches of the *sssss*urface dwellers," said Skales. "We live as a peaceful society now."

"Really?" Pythor flashed a toothy smile. "You wouldn't be interested in, say, a sneak peek of the BorgWatch?"

"Did someone say 'BorgWatch?'" a little voice cried out from behind them.

A young snake approached them. He bore a striking resemblance to Skales.

"Skales Junior!" Skales yelled at his son. "You *ssssh*ould be home with your mother."

"But Daddy, I've been reading about the BorgWatch." Skales Junior whipped out a copy of *Tech Times* magazine. "This article says the BorgWatch is going to have a built-in video game application that lets you play *Snake Attack* in 3-D!"

"Smart kid you've got there," said Pythor. "He clearly understands the importance of what I'm offering you."

More and more snakes began slithering over. They surrounded Pythor, Skales, and Skales Junior.

"If he ha*ssss* something to *ssssh*ow us, let him *sssssh*ow us," hissed a Hypnobrai.

"Ye*sssssss*," a Venomari added. "I, too, would like a *sssssss*neak peek of the BorgWatch."

"All right," Skales finally said to Pythor. "What is it you have that is *ssssss*so important?"

Pythor slid up onto a nearby stone wall, clearly relishing the attention. "Ladies and gentle-snakes, I present to you the first-ever, never-before-seen, I-am-definitely-the-*first*-one-to-be-revealing-this, look at . . . the BorgWatch Thermodynamic Temperature Gauge!"

With a flourish, Pythor held up the temperature gauge high for all to see.

The crowd murmured.

"It'*sssssss* a toothpick," called out the Hypnobrai.

"No, no," insisted Pythor. "I assure you, you snakes are the FIRST to see this exclusive look at the BorgWatch Thermodynamic Temperature Gauge. Courtesy of me, Pythor P. Chumsworth."

The murmurs turned to confused rumbles.

"But what does*sssss* it do?" a snake asked.

"Ah, an astute question," Pythor said. "Allow me to demonstrate the power of this amazing body temperature control system. Observe." Pythor turned his attention to the

metal toothpick. He looked at the top. He looked at the bottom. He tapped it.

"Hmmmmm," he said. "Well, if it had a display screen, I'm sure it would be easier to understand."

Unimpressed, the snakes began slithering away.

"Wait, wait!" cried Pythor. "Don't you see? This will revolutionize the way we live! Look, it's reading my internal temperature now. At least, I think it is . . ."

"I knew you could be desssssperate, Pythor," said Skales. "But thisssss is ridiculoussssss."

"Hang on," said Skales Junior, coming closer for a better look. "It *does* look like something I saw on the BorgWatch Watch Blog. It was only a rumor. But maybe if we plug it into my BorgPad, it will work."

Just then, the doors to the snake village swung open, and the ninja burst in on a wave of Spinjitzu!

"NINJA-GO!" Their voices echoed through the caverns.

"Ahhhhh!" all the snakes cried, scattering. "We're under attack from the surface dwellers!"

"No — no, this isn't an attack!" Lloyd assured them. "There's only one snake we're after."

"And it's that con artist right there!" yelled Jay, pointing at Pythor.

"Rats." Pythor groaned as the ninja spotted him. "Time to hightail it out of here."

In a whirlwind of Spinjitzu, the ninja chased Pythor around the village. They flew across the marketplace, up over rooftops, and back through the tunnels up toward the surface.

Skales shook his head as he watched them go.

"Daddy?" asked Skales Junior. "Can I go up to the surface now to wait for the BorgWatch reveal?"

"No, *sssssss*on," Skales said. "Tru*sssssss*t me. They're crazy up there."

Chapter 7

Give it up, Pythor!" yelled Lloyd as they chased him up the ladder to the surface.

"Never!" cried Pythor. "I *will* reveal this to the masses!"

Lloyd looked over at Zane. "Let's put him on ice."

Zane nodded. "Agreed!" He quickly targeted the manhole cover and shot an ice blast around the rim. The manhole was sealed shut!

"Hah! That'll cool him off!" cheered Jay.

Pythor scowled. But, suddenly, the toothpick in his hand began to glow.

"Adjusting thermodynamic range for optimal conditions," it announced from a microscopic speaker. "Heating in three, two, one . . ."

Pythor yelped as the toothpick glowed red-hot! It let out a heat blast that melted Zane's ice!

Everyone blinked.

"It can do that?" asked Cole.

"Apparently," said Zane.

Pythor's scowl turned to a triumphant sneer. "Nifty little gadget. If you'll excuse me, I have a crowd to share this with."

"No!" cried the ninja as Pythor zipped up and out of the manhole into the streets above.

"Come on, guys!" yelled Lloyd. "We can't let him reach the fans!"

One by one, the ninja leaped out of the manhole and into the streets of Ninjago City. The crowd outside the BorgStore had grown even larger during the time they'd been underground.

"Where did Pythor go?" Kai asked, scanning the crowd.

"There!" Jay pointed to the snake, who was scaling a lamppost. "Come on!"

As the ninja scrambled to catch up, Pythor reached the top of the lamppost and yelled as loudly as he could. "Citizens of Ninjago City! I have here in my possession a sneak peek of the BorgWatch!"

"Who is that guy?" a woman asked.

Her companion rolled his eyes. "Just another loony looking for attention. The city is swimming with 'em these days. Just last night, I saw some crackpot dressed like a stone warrior outside the museum. I'm tellin' ya, they're comin' out of the woodwork."

The woman shook her head. "A shame what this city is coming to."

But Pythor wasn't deterred. "If you'll please all just listen to me for one moment, you'll see that I have the exact thing you're waiting for — a piece of the BorgWatch itself."

"Yeah right, buddy," called a man in a ball cap. "And I'm the Golden Master."

People in the crowd laughed.

"It isn't working," Jay whispered to his friends. "They don't believe him."

But a glint came to Pythor's eye. "Who here reads the BorgWatch Watch Blog?" he asked loudly.

Almost every hand in the audience went up.

"Then I'm sure you've all read the rumors of the BorgWatch Thermodynamic Temperature Gauge," said Pythor. "Well, allow me, Pythor P. Chumsworth, to present you with proof that the rumors are true, and I do indeed have the very first sneak peek of that revolutionary BorgWatch component. Observe!"

Pythor held the metal toothpick up to his forehead.

"Internal body temperature within optimal levels," the toothpick said loudly through its microscopic speaker.

That got people's attention.

"The BorgWatch Watch Blog did say the temperature gauge would be incredibly small," a man in a suit commented to his friend. "As small as a toothpick."

"I saw in *Tech Times* magazine that Borg was tinkering with microscopic speakers," another fan said. He was dressed up like Cyrus Borg, wheelchair and all.

"If that toothpick is part of the BorgWatch, then how did you get hold of it?" someone called.

Pythor's eyes flashed. "Let's just say I have my sources."

Members of the crowd began to murmur.

"If it's real, let us see it!" a woman with a small dog yelled.

"*Arf, arf!*" barked her dog.

"Uh-oh," Kai whispered to his friends. "This is turning on us. We've got to do something."

"But what?" asked Cole. "We can't stop thousands of BorgWatch groupies. Not as long as they believe him."

A determined look crossed Lloyd's face. "Then let's give them a reason to doubt," he said. "Come on! Zane, I'm going to need your help."

Meanwhile, Pythor was busy soaking in the attention of the fans.

"Now, now, not all at once," he said as the people drew closer. "Folks with cameras are allowed to take selfies with me first. Perhaps someone with a BorgPad might be so kind as to allow me to demonstrate the sheer power of this BorgWatch temperature gauge."

But just then, everyone's attention was diverted to a loud voice from another lamppost.

"Check it out!" Lloyd bellowed. "A sneak peek of the first BorgWatch component leaked to the public — the BorgWatch Thermodynamic Temperature Gauge!"

Lloyd held up a small microchip for everyone to see. Then he winked at Zane, who

was standing below. Using his own speaker system, Zane projected a loud message.

"Internal body temperature within optimal levels," Zane's speaker said.

"Hey, I thought the guy in the snake costume had the BorgWatch Thermodynamic Temperature Gauge," a woman called.

"Yeah, what's going on?" asked the business suit guy.

Pythor waved his hands wildly. "Never mind them! They are simply copycats. Mine is the real thing!"

Suddenly, Nya was atop another lamppost. "Hey, Borg fanatics, get a load of this!" she cried. "The first ever sneak peek of the new BorgWatch InstaMusic Party Starter! Check it out!"

Nya held up a plain metal ring. Again, Zane used his speakers to make it sound like the ring was playing funky party music loud enough for the whole crowd to hear.

Now people were extremely confused.

"Why are all these people saying they have pieces of the BorgWatch?" a guy asked.

"You haven't heard?" Kai replied innocently. "Some con artist over on Main Street is selling fake BorgWatch pieces and telling people they're real. And these bozos think they can get their fifteen minutes of fame by showing them off. Unbelievable. I even heard that that girl with the 'party speaker' didn't even know what a Cyrus PDA was until this morning."

Pythor looked around in alarm as the crowd began to turn on him and the ninja.

"No, no, *mine* is real!" Pythor screamed. "It's the others who are lying to you!"

But the fans had made up their minds. They roughly shoved Pythor, Lloyd, and Nya out of the crowd.

"Don't waste our time with fake leaks," the man in the ball cap said.

"Yeah — Fluffy here doesn't take kindly

56

to misinformation!" the woman with the snapped.

"*Grrrrrrrrrrrr!*" Fluffy growled.

In all the commotion, it was tough to see who ended up where. But after a few moments, Nya, Zane, and Lloyd came tumbling out of the crowd.

Kai, Cole, and Jay ran up to them.

"Guys, that was awesome!" cried Cole. "Now people will never buy Pythor's story."

"Indeed," said Zane. "The chances of his success are now extremely small, barring unforeseen conditions."

"Good job, team," said Lloyd. "Now, all that's left is to get the temperature gauge and head to Dr. Saunders . . ."

The ninja all suddenly looked around.

"Oh, no!" moaned Nya. "Where did that snake slither off to this time?"

In the excitement, the ninja had lost track of Pythor. He had escaped again!

Chapter 8

Back on board the *Destiny's Bounty*, the ninja paced back and forth along the bridge. Jay flipped through television channels, pulling up the afternoon programs.

"There's got to be a way to track that snake down," said Kai angrily.

"Without information on his next plan, we have no way of calculating where he will go," said Zane.

"Tell me again what he has that's so important?" Misako asked the ninja. She and Master Wu had joined them on the bridge.

"Pythor has the BorgWatch Thermodynamic Temperature Gauge," said Zane.

Nya sighed. "It's a toothpick. It's *literally* a metal toothpick."

"That we all signed contracts to protect," groaned Cole.

"I believe you mean nondisclosure agreements," Zane observed.

Lloyd shook his head. "Now's not the time, buddy. And it's not about the contracts, anyway. It's about keeping our promise."

"You're forgetting something, Lloyd," Kai said. "It's also about not letting that sneaky snake get the better of us!"

Meanwhile, the television blared in the background. "This just in, the BorgWatch crowd grows ever larger," a reporter was saying. "Campers are being asked to please bring their own restroom facilities, as it looks like the campout may last well into the week."

"Jay, could you turn that down?" asked Kai, annoyed.

Jay didn't answer. He was completely focused on the screen, flipping from news channel to news channel.

Kai sighed and looked to the others. "Maybe the problem will resolve itself. Once the BorgWatch is unveiled, no one will care about Pythor's stupid thermo-gizmo."

"But we don't know if the watch is even being revealed this week," said Nya. "That gives Pythor a lot of time to shop around."

"Well, there's got to be a way to track him —" Cole started. But he was interrupted by an annoying jingle promoting Gayle Gossip's evening talk show.

"For the gossip that's the juiciest you'll ever find, watch the Gayle Gossip show, every weekday night at nine!"

"Jay, seriously, SHUT IT OFF!" yelled Cole.

But Jay jumped to his feet. "There!" he cried. "Got him!"

Sure enough, Gayle Gossip came on the screen. And beside her was Pythor!

"Join me for what may be the biggest gossip we've ever spilled," Gayle Gossip gushed. "For the first time *ever*, we have exclusively obtained a sneak peek of . . . the BorgWatch! Coming up on my show tonight at nine."

The ninja gasped.

"Jay, you're a genius!" cried Nya. "How'd you know to search for Pythor on the news?"

Jay grinned. "When you're as big a Borg gadget fan as I am, you know where the rumor leaks are going to be."

"Come on!" said Lloyd. "We've got to get down to the studio and steal back that temperature gauge before the show goes live!"

Six shadows crept along the back alleyway of Gayle Gossip's studio building. A security guard passed by, and one by one the shadows disappeared behind a pile of crates.

"There it is," Kai whispered, lowering his mask. "The backstage doors."

The ninja eyed the security guard as he stood watch over the entrance.

"We need to get in there unseen," said Jay. "Shouldn't be too hard for six trained ninja."

Suddenly, Cole's cell phone buzzed loudly. Cole scrambled to silence it.

"Cole, could you *please* shut that off?" Kai snapped.

"It's not my fault!" Cole complained. "I keep getting automated calls from Borg's legal team asking about the temperature gauge leak. Listen!"

Cole played the message quietly for his friends to hear.

"This is an automated message from Cyrus Borg's Legal Advantage team. Please be advised that you have signed a binding nondisclosure agreement pertaining to sensitive Borg Industries materials. Recent

reports indicate a potential breach in agreement. Any breach will result in fines, penalties, and jail time. Press 'one' to confirm receipt of this message. Press 'two' if you are actively ignoring our attempts to contact you."

"See?!" Cole hissed. "They've left me seven messages already!"

"Well, turn it off, then," said Lloyd. "Let's take care of this once and for all."

The ninja nodded and raised their hoods. *"Ninja-GO!"* they whispered.

The friends slipped up alongside the building. Just then, the security guard's walkie-talkie buzzed.

"You there, Dan?" a voice came through. "Think I forgot my socks at home again. Can I borrow your backup pair?"

Jay quietly zapped a tiny jolt of electricity at the walkie-talkie.

Dan the security guard went to respond. "Yeah, sure, they're in my locker, over."

But the walkie-talkie buzzed with static. "Yo — ere —an?" the speaker garbled. "Really — eed —ocks."

Dan sighed. "All right. I'm on my way."

The ninja watched as Dan headed though the double doors to backstage. Quickly, Kai used a small burst of fire to melt the door's lock before it closed. The six ninja slipped into the studio unseen.

Inside, television crew members were hurrying this way and that preparing for the evening's show. Beyond the stage curtains, the ninja could see the studio audience already seated, eagerly awaiting the BorgWatch "sneak peek."

"Now, you're sure what you're telling me is legit?" The voice belonged to Gayle Gossip. The ninja watched her walk by with Pythor.

"Trust me," Pythor said smoothly. "I proved it to your producers myself. The Borg Industries seal. Its capabilities are obvious once it's plugged into a BorgPad. It's all there. There's

no denying the BorgWatch Thermodynamic Temperature Gauge is authentic."

Gayle nodded. "Normally I check these things out myself, but there's no time. Not with the unveiling happening any day now. And Fred Finley is absolutely *killing* me in the ratings. We need this promotional boost if we're going to stay in the game."

Pythor smiled charmingly. "Not to worry. Tonight's reveal will put me — I mean, *you* — back in the spotlight."

Just then, an assistant rushed up to apply fresh powder to Gayle's face.

"Tell the team I want the Thermodynamic Temperature Gauge on my desk in five," Gayle instructed her.

"Right!" chirped the assistant. "I'll have them bring it from the safe."

The six ninja watched Gayle's assistant scamper off.

"That's our cue," said Lloyd. "It's showtime!"

Chapter 9

The ninja followed Gayle's assistant down the hall.

"Quick, put these on!" Nya whispered, snatching several stagehand uniforms from a rack.

Dressed like the crew, the ninja had no problem blending in. In fact, no one seemed to notice them at all. Everyone was too busy getting ready for the show.

Outside the storage room, Gayle's assistant spoke to a prop guard. "Gayle wants the thermo-thingo," she said. "I need it from the safe."

The guard nodded and went back into the storage room.

In a flash, Nya zipped up alongside the assistant.

"There you are!" she said in a haughty voice. "We've been looking everywhere. Gayle needs you — NOW!"

The assistant looked flustered.

"But . . . but I just saw her. She told me to go get the —"

"Do you *really* think that's what she wants you to get right now?" Nya huffed. "That's the prop guy's job. Your job is to make sure she has what *she* needs."

"But I — I . . ." the assistant stammered.

"Go, go, GO!" Nya shouted, propelling her down the hallway.

Confused, the assistant hurried off.

Just then, the prop guard returned, holding a small box.

"Where'd Gayle's assistant go?" he asked. "She needed this."

"There was an emergency," said Nya. "She asked us to take it for her."

Without waiting for a reply, Nya snagged the box from the guard. "Thanks!" she said brightly. Then she joined the others around the corner.

"That was awesome!" Jay said proudly.

Nya winked and carefully opened the box. The Thermodynamic Temperature Gauge was inside!

"I don't believe it," Kai whispered. "That was . . . easy!"

Lloyd took the temperature gauge from the box and examined it quickly. "Let's just be glad it was that easy and get out of here," he said. "Before —"

"YOU!!!"

The ninja whipped around to find an enraged Pythor staring them down.

"I knew I couldn't trust you to stay away!" Pythor hissed angrily. "Never send an assistant to do a snake's job!"

"Yeah, well this time, the show's over," said Lloyd, snapping the box shut.

"Indeed," hissed Pythor. "It's curtains for you!"

Pythor lashed out with his staff and whacked the box from Lloyd's hands. But this time, Jay was ready. He used a well-aimed jolt of electricity to zap the box back toward him. Jay grabbed it!

"Let's Spinjitzu out of here!" exclaimed Kai.

"Negative," said Zane. "There are too many bystanders. Someone could get hurt."

"Plus, they'll know it's us and we'll get arrested for stealing back the stupid thing we'll get arrested for losing in the first place," exclaimed Cole.

"Then it looks like we're escaping the old-fashioned way," said Lloyd. "Run!"

The ninja turned and hightailed it down the hallway. Pythor slithered after them. They sped past startled assistants, sending refreshment trays flying.

"Excuse us! Coming through!" Cole yelled. "Pardon us. Sorry 'bout that. Ooh — a donut!"

That gave him an idea. "We may not be able to use Spinjitzu, but we can have a ... FOOD FIGHT!"

Cole nabbed a plate of fruit and chucked it back behind them. Apples, peaches, and bananas went flying.

Pythor was moving too quickly to avoid it — he slipped on the banana peels and went sailing through the air.

"Good thinking, Cole!" said Lloyd. "We're almost — whoa!!"

At that moment, an oversized prop gurney crossed the hall right in front of the ninja. They careened headlong into it! Heavy props scattered everywhere.

"Ugh!" groaned Jay, pushing a planter box off his legs. He shook his head and held up the temperature gauge box. It was undamaged. "That was close," he said. "Is everyone okay?"

"Heh, heh, heh." came a voice from behind the ninja.

They turned to discover Pythor holding the rope to a heavy bunch of sandbags hanging from the ceiling. He had them poised to fall right on top of Zane, who was pinned under a heavy prop!

"Hand over the goods," Pythor sneered. "Or the Titanium Ninja goes *crunch*."

"Lloyd, quick!" yelled Jay. "Use your power to stop the sandbags!"

Lloyd shook his head. "I can't. It's not safe. We have no choice. Give him the temperature gauge."

"What are you talking about?" cried Jay. "Desperate times call for — just use your power!"

But Lloyd shook his head vehemently.

The sound of footsteps echoed from around the corner. The entire crew of the show was bearing down on them.

"There's no time, Jay. Just give it to him!"

Torn, Jay chucked the box to Pythor.

The snake laughed as he caught it with his tail ... and released the sandbags anyway!

"No!" cried Jay. He lunged forward and grabbed Zane. Amazingly, the heavy prop pinning him down seemed to grow lighter, and Jay was able to pull his friend away easily.

Jay and Zane both rolled out of the way a moment before the bags smashed to the ground. Sand exploded everywhere, filling the air.

"Quick!" Lloyd called through the cloud. "We have to escape — now!"

Following Lloyd's lead, the ninja dashed out the backstage double doors before Gayle Gossip's crew could spot them leaving through the cloud of dust.

Kai melted the lock on the door behind them. Everyone coughed.

"I don't believe it," Jay groaned. "We had the temperature gauge in our hands, and now it's about to go live on national television."

"What a catastrophe," Nya groaned. "Okay, everyone, what do we do now? Anyone have any brilliant ideas?"

Lloyd winked . . . and pulled out the Thermodynamic Temperature Gauge from under his sleeve!

"Because it had to look convincing," he said.

"Is that . . ." started Jay.

"The temperature gauge!" cried Kai. "I've never been so happy to see a metal toothpick!"

"When Pythor spotted us, I swapped it out for an ordinary piece of metal I brought from the *Bounty*," Lloyd explained. "I had a feeling we'd never get that snake to give up on his fifteen minutes of fame. So I took

a page from his playbook and changed tactics."

"Do you mean Pythor's about to go on television and reveal a normal metal toothpick that can't do anything?" asked Kai.

Lloyd shrugged. "Well, I guess it *can* clean his teeth."

"That's why the prop was so light when I grabbed Zane!" Jay realized. "You used your powers after all!"

"Yup!" said Lloyd.

"A very logical decision," Zane said approvingly.

The ninja all laughed.

"Let's head home to the *Bounty*'s big-screen television," said Kai. "I want to watch the look on Pythor's face when he realizes what's happened. In HD."

Chapter 10

The next morning, the ninja headed to the Ninjago Museum of History. They chatted about Gayle Gossip's show the night before.

Pythor was livid when he realized he'd been duped. Luckily, Gayle Gossip made it look like revealing a fake piece of the BorgWatch was planned all along.

Some fans were angry. Others thought it was hysterical. But after all was said and done, Pythor's "fifteen minutes of fame" ended up turning into nothing more than a blip on page fifteen of the *Daily Dish* tabloid.

"I'll never forget the look on his face when Gayle pretended to clean her teeth with the toothpick." Jay cracked up. "Priceless!"

The ninja stepped through the Kozu-shaped hole in the wall to find Dr. Saunders bustling around the museum storage room, gathering space heaters and blankets.

"Ah, ninja!" the doctor exclaimed. "I was wondering where you were being. You said you would have the parts to fix my thermostat yesterday, yes? The temperature is all wrong! It must to be fixed immediately."

"Do not worry, doctor." Zane stepped forward. "We have come with the replacement part, as promised."

Using his Nindroid expertise, Zane quickly fused the Thermodynamic Temperature Gauge into Dr. Saunders's broken thermostat. The technology melded perfectly, and the thermostat kicked on once more.

"Hooray!" cheered the ninja.

"Oh, thanking goodness." Dr. Saunders dropped the heap of blankets.

"Pretty nifty little piece of technology, huh, doc?" Jay asked happily.

To his surprise, the doctor scowled.

"I despise technology," Dr. Saunders said.

The ninja blinked. But the cloud passed from Dr. Saunders's face as quickly as it had appeared. "But I am supposing that for once, yes, it is of benefit. Keeping all the corridors in the museum at perfect temperature."

"Actually, it's kind of warm in here." Kai tugged at his collar. "It's starting to feel like a sauna in here. Zane, maybe check that the temperature gauge is working right."

"No, no, it is working fine," Dr. Saunders assured them. "Perfect comfort. Just right for base — I mean, museum patrons! Now, if you'll excuse me, I have much to clean."

Lloyd looked around at the mess still remaining from Dareth's fight with Kozu.

"Guys, we have to help Dr. Saunders clean up his museum," he said. "It's only right."

"More work?" groaned Jay.

The ninja gave him a look.

Jay sighed. "Fine. I'll get the mop."

As they were leaving, Zane noticed a large hourglass sitting on a high shelf.

"That is an interesting antique, Dr. Saunders," Zane commented. "It appears to be the only glass item that did not shatter."

Dr. Saunders followed Zane's gaze. "Ah, yes, indeed," he said, nodding slowly. "A very old hourglass. Very special."

Dr. Saunders ushered the ninja out from the storage room. Before he left as well, he turned to look up at the hourglass.

"Very special," he repeated quietly. "I've been marking time by it for many years now."

Only Dr. Saunders recognized a hum in the museum basement vibrating through the storage room floor.

He smiled. Then he shut the door.